The Pearl
of
Great Price

By

John C Burt

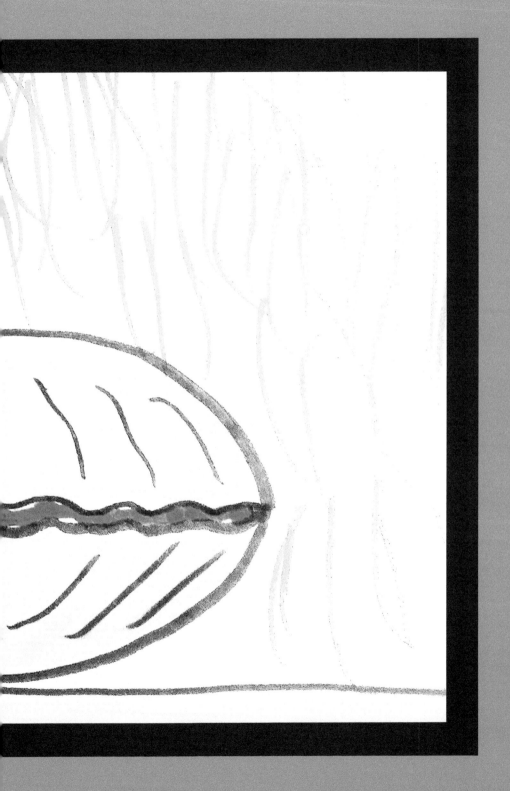

There once was an oyster named Oscar who lived on the bottom of the Pacific Ocean. Most of the time Oscar kept his

shell closed ...
One could not too
careful because
there were
predators in the
deep ocean .....

11

Yet when Oscar did open his shell and reveal what was inside of it ... One could only be amazed and have wonder and awe . Because Oscar within the insides of his shell had the biggest and largest and greatest pearl one could ever see.

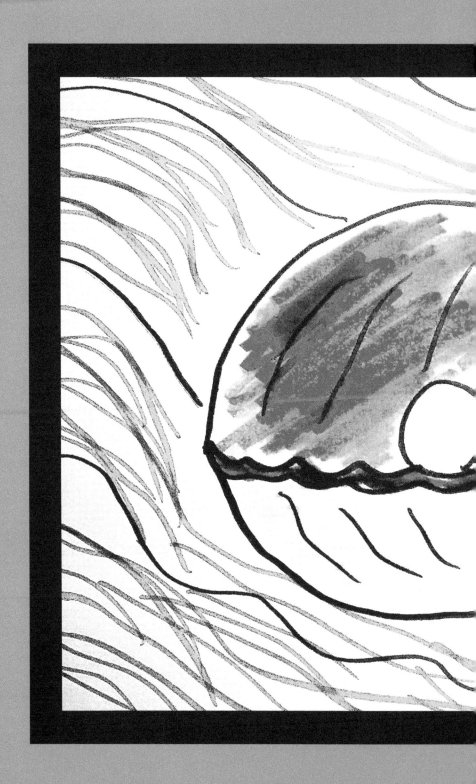

The news about
what Oscar had
inside his shell
had spread ... Even
to the world above
the waves of the
ocean ..... Many a

treasure - hunter came seeking to take the pearl of great price from Oscar ... None had yet succeeded .. yet they still tried and tried to get the

pearl of great
price from within
Oscar and his
shell. .....Oscar was
on the bottom of
the deepest of
deepest ocean

depths .... There were a lot of fish who traveled the highways and byways of the ocean depths near Oscar ....

The people of above the waves wanted to display the pearl of great price in a red velvet box . Which of course

Oscar had no knowledge of ..... Oscar just instead noticed that the number of people from above the waves kept increasing ....

More and more people coming from above the waves .... all seeking to possess the pearl of great price from Oscar..

But what the people from above the waves did not know was Oscar had family. Each oyster had a pearl of great price .....

Lightning Source UK Ltd.
Milton Keynes UK
UKHW022327170119
335685UK00001B/5/P